THE ADVENTURES
OF
MINKY AND BEE

By Denise Mullenary

Illustrated By T. J. Morales

Mullenary Books – Lompoc, CA

ISBN: 978-0-578-59035-6

For my children,

may you always find your adventure.

"I love you more"-Mom

In a town near a meadow
with flowers and trees,
there lives two young sisters,
named Minky and Bee.

They love to explore and be brave,
come what may;
An exciting adventure awaits them each day.

Now, Minky is small and a little bit thin,
with a pretty pink dress and a scrape on her shin.
She sings while she skips and her walk is a run;
her wispy brown hair is pulled back in a bun.
Loving learning and books, she's incredibly bright;
using "yes please" and "thank you", she's always polite.

Bee is quite small, yet more round in the tummy;
she loves to eat snacks and all things that are yummy.
Her smile is so big it shines out through her eyes;
bright yellow shorts showcase rolls in her thighs.
Her dark head of hair is so wavy and curled;
she looks up to her sister the most in the world.

The day  Bee was born Minky spoke in her ear;

"I'll love you forever, we're best friends, you hear?
I will teach you things that I know and someday,
When you're bigger I'll take you outside and we'll play!
There's a secret place with a magical tree,
Let's go on adventures there, just you and me."

As time

quickly passed

and the years

rolled on by;

Minky taught Bee

to crawl, to walk,

and to fly!

She introduced her to "Bubba the Bear",
a little stuffed teddy with much wear and tear.
Bee loved this teddy named Bubba so much,
she hugged him all day, he was so soft to touch.

Since Minky shared Bubba, Mom gave her a box;
inside it she found a new red velvet fox.
They named the fox Scarlett and knew she was wise;
with a white bushy tail and shiny black eyes.

Soon Scarlett and Bubba and Minky and Bee,
hike down to the meadow surrounded by trees.

Down the road, cross the stream, they know the way;
for they travel it seamlessly most every day.

Just past the bridge grew an oak with a hole,
they crawl on all fours in the dark like a mole.

Through this magical tree all their troubles faded;
whatever their minds could dream up now awaited.

Bubba Bear and Miss Fox
now become life size;
The first time it happened
was quite the surprise!
They can walk on two legs,
tell jokes, and have fun;
they play with the girls
in the bright summer sun.
While Miss Scarlett the Fox
is stylish and smart,
Bubba loves to be silly and
laughs at a fart.

The colors of flowers and smell of the land,
seem brighter and sweeter, so vivid and grand.
In this place their imagination runs wild;
they can be free and love every day as a child.

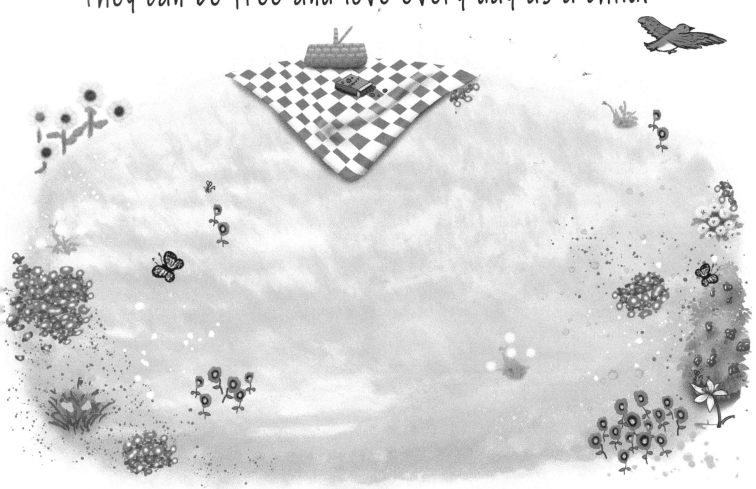

They meet Giants and Fairies
on one of their quests.
They see birds that build large
and elaborate nests.

Mermaid tails grow when
they swim in the creek.
There is treasure to find,
and animals speak.

Bee soars through the clouds
on a horse that has wings;
Minky sounds like an Angel
whenever she sings.

Bubba builds a fine swing
with some rope and a tire;
Scarlett pushes them round
as they squeal and shout,
"higher!"

Fighting pirates with swords on an old wooden ship,

they stand on the tree trunk and try not to slip.

"Walk the plank!" Captain yells, and they quiver with fear,

for they know that these waters have crocodiles near.

As they jump off the plank and roll down through the

grass, they imagine a speed boat and step on the gas.

As the sky becomes pink
and the day turns to dusk,
they lean back and slide
down an elephant tusk.
While hugging his trunk they
see eyes full of sorrow;
they smile and promise to
come back tomorrow.

In the distance they hear Mama calling their names,
so they run to the tree to leave all of their games.
They crawl through the hole and brush off the dirt,
then cross the bridge slowly so no one gets hurt.

Bubba, now stuffed, is up high on Bee's shoulders;
his fur keeps her warm as the air becomes colder.

At home they throw Fox and Bear in the cradle;
wash off their hands and sit down at the table.
Daddy loosens his tie and blesses the food;
together they talk and enjoy the warm mood.

Though Minky and Bee love their time to go play,
this family time is the best part of their day.

Once dinner is done they help Mom with the dishes;
She asks them about all their hopes, dreams, and wishes.

They tromp up the stairs and lay down in their beds;
Dad reads them a story and kisses their heads.

He pulls back the curtain and shows them the moon;

some fireflies dance to a cricket's sweet tune.

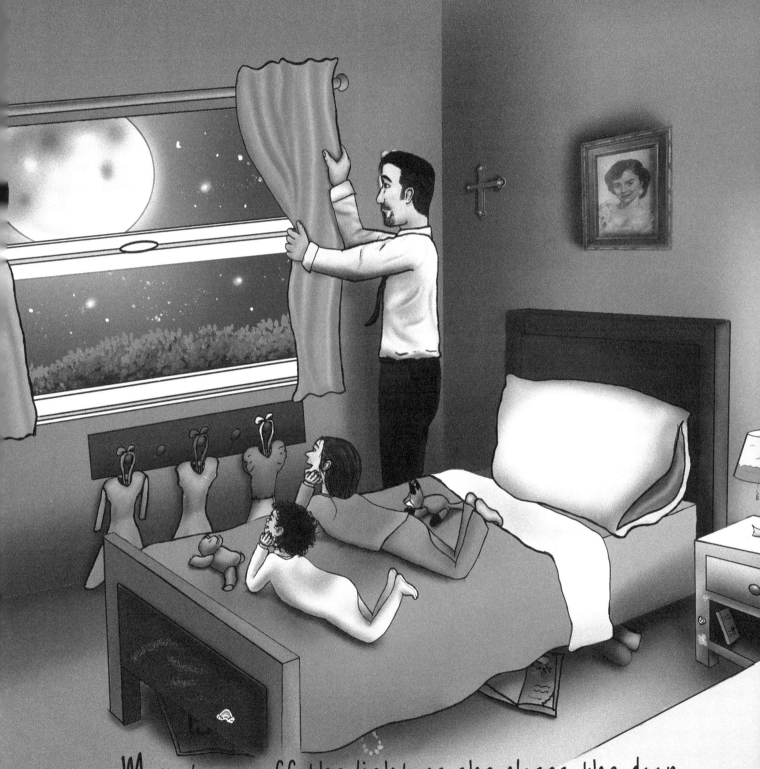

Mom turns off the light as she closes the door.

Tomorrow awaits them adventures galore!

Bee rolls in her bed and whispers to Minky,

(who lifts up her pillow and pulls out a binkie),

"I had such a great time in the meadow, my friend.

We will play there forever, until it's...

The End."

COLOR WITH ME
Ask your parents if they can copy this page and print one for you to color!
Feel free to post your creation on Facebook: "Denise Mullenary Author" for
everyone to see!

Look and Find

Can you find these pictures along our adventure?

About the Author - Denise Mullenary

Denise is a happily married mother of four children.
She enjoys reading, writing, and a good cup of coffee!

The book characters, Scarlett, Bubba, Minky, and Bee each represent one of her own kids and their unique personalities. The lily flower throughout the book is for her beautiful niece, Lily.

Stay tuned for the next book in the Minky and Bee Adventure series, Mermaid Mission: A Shell for Nell, available for purchase in 2020.

Denise Mullenary can be contacted at mullenarybooks@gmail.com and followed on social media for updates on book release and signings.
Facebok: Denise Mullenary Author

About the Illustrator - T. J. Morales

Illustrator Thomas J. Morales lives in a small town on the central coast of California with his dog, Bubbie. He loves his big family and as a Christian he draws inspiration from his faith.

He started his career taking art courses at Allan Hancock College and building his skills and knowledge of multiple art mediums.

This book has been a joy to work on and there's more on the way! Instagram @tjmorales09